ALWAYS COME

HOME TO ME

Belle Yang

CANDLEWICK PRESS
CAMBRIDGE, MASSACHUSETTS

First edition 2007

Library of Congress Cataloging-in-Publication Data
Yang, Belle.
Always come home to me / Belle Yang. — 1st ed.
p. cm.
Summary: A pair of young twins, living with their parents in a small
town in northern China, are devastated when the doves they love and care
for are given to their uncle and determine to find a way to get them back.
ISBN 978-0-7636-2899-4
[1. Pigeons—Fiction. 2. Brothers and sisters—Fiction.
3. Twins—Fiction. 4. China—Fiction.] I. Title.
PZ7.Y1925Alw 2007
[E]—dc22   2007060858

2 4 6 8 10 9 7 5 3 1

Printed in China

This book was typeset in Barbador.
The illustrations were done in gouache.

Candlewick Press
2067 Massachusetts Avenue
Cambridge, Massachusetts 02140

visit us at www.candlewick.com

For a few Candlewick kids, big and small—
Owen Wayland Magoon, John Henry McMillan,
Jonathan Perez-Reyzin, Mae Elise Pawlikowski,
and Nathaniel Santoro

IN A FARAWAY CORNER of northern China, at the meeting of two rivers, in the town of He-Ping, up a crooked path, Mei-Mei and her twin brother, Di-Di, lived with their *mama* and *baba.*

Mama and Baba loved their children dearly. When Mei-Mei and Di-Di walked through the gate each morning on their way to school, Mama called out, *"Fei, fei*—fly, fly, little birds, but always come home to me!"

On the day of Ching Ming Festival, a joyful day
in spring when families sweep their ancestors' graves,
some cousins gave the twins a present— something they
had longed for—a pair of young doves. Mei-Mei rocked
the female in her arms. Di-Di stroked the feathers of the
bigger male, who cried, *Hrruu-hrruu.*

"Boy and girl twins just like us," said Di-Di. "Let's
name the girl Butterfly."

"And let's call the boy Squeaky," Mei-Mei said with
a giggle, "because he complains like you."

The children built a dovecote out of orange crates.
They set it on the window ledge to keep the birds safe
from weasels. Each morning the children padded
the dovecote with clean, sweet hay.

Mei-Mei and Di-Di fed the birds as gently

as Mama and Baba had spoon-fed them when

they were small.

When the cherry blossoms began to spring

open like popcorn, the birds' wing feathers had

grown long. Mei-Mei and Di-Di bounced the birds

in their palms and urged them to fly. When the

birds took to the air, the children's hearts soared.

When the birds landed clumsily in the persimmon

tree, they laughed.

By the time yellow flowers were blossoming on the melon vines, the children were racing their doves on the wind.

"*Fei, fei*—fly, fly, little birds," called Mei-Mei.

"But always come home to me!" cried Di-Di, fearful of hawks, which prey on doves and other small birds.

Whenever the twins trilled—*trr!*—the doves flew down from the clouds and lit safely on their shoulders. Mei-Mei and Di-Di felt as if Butterfly and Squeaky had chosen them, above all other people, to be their friends and protectors.

One day at dawn, late in the summer, Uncle Baldy came from faraway Dog Willow to help Baba harvest his fields. The two men worked into the afternoon, never stopping for lunch. The horizon was dark with rain clouds.

"Elder Brother," said Uncle Baldy as they rested under the grape arbor, "those doves of yours—I'd sure like to have them on my farm."

"For your help today, Baldy," said Baba, "I am very grateful. The birds are yours."

When they returned home from school that day and learned that their doves had been given away to Uncle Baldy, Mei-Mei and Di-Di wanted to run to catch up with him. But their uncle's wagon was by then beyond the next village.

At supper, Mei-Mei couldn't slurp down her noodles. Di-Di's tears plopped into his bowl. Baba was not there to see his children's pale faces. He remained busy in the fields, racing against the coming storm.

Uncle Baldy returned two evenings later after he had been to market with his vegetables. He would have a cup of tea with Baba before continuing home to Dog Willow.

"*Lai-ba* — come on, Di-Di," said Mei-Mei. "We'll hide in the wagon."

The children lifted the tarp on their uncle's wagon and crawled underneath. A cricket chirped shrilly in a corner and made them jump.

After a while, Baba called, *"Zai jian!* Good-bye, Baldy!" The wagon swayed as Uncle Baldy climbed aboard. *"Jiarr!"* Uncle Baldy said to his horse, and the wheels began to turn, squeaking, *Gaaa-zi, gaa-zi.*

The road to Dog Willow was bumpy, and the children's bottoms grew sore as the night grew old. Clouds swallowed up the harvest moon. Though their teeth chattered and their stomachs growled, Mei-Mei and Di-Di finally nodded off.

They were awakened by the GOO-LOO-LOONG of thunder. Uncle Baldy's hand reached under the tarp and nearly brushed Di-Di's face as he groped for his rain hat and coat. Di-Di thought he was going to sneeze!

Many hours later, the wagon came to a full stop. A rough hand threw off the tarp. The east was silver like the belly of a fish. They had arrived at Uncle Baldy's farm.

"*Wha!* Mei-Mei! Di-Di!" cried Uncle Baldy. "Aiya! What are you doing here? Your *baba* and *mama* must be sick with worry!"

"Uncle Baldy, if you'll let us see our doves," said Mei-Mei, "we'll help you grind the corn here on the farm."

"Yah, we'll brush your burros and mules, too," said Di-Di. "We'll do anything you ask!"

Uncle Baldy's scowl melted into a smile. "I can see how much you miss your doves," he said, and scratched his head. "Let's go get them!" The children cheered as they climbed down and followed their uncle to the barn.

"My heavens, it's Mei-Mei and Di-Di!" said Auntie Li-Li, at the well.

"Oh, Auntie, we came for our doves!" cried the children.

"I'm so sorry, my darlings," said Auntie Li-Li, "but the birds disappeared from the barn just before dawn." She gently stroked the twins' faces. "They may have been scared off by owls."

"Or by hawks," said Mei-Mei under her breath.

She and Di-Di had come all this way, only to find that their birds were gone!

The return journey that night was miserable. Mei-Mei and Di-Di had nothing to look forward to except Baba's spanking.

The fragrance of breakfast porridge was wafting through the gate when the children arrived home. Uncle Baldy continued on to the market.

"You go in first," said Di-Di.

"Maybe we should find hay to pad our bottoms," said Mei-Mei.

They pushed open the gate, just a crack, and slipped inside. The dog came barking. Mama heard and rushed out into the yard.

"My sweet sparrows!" she cried. The children fell, sobbing, into her arms, which smelled of fresh dough.

"Your father didn't sleep at all," said Mama. "He walked every lane and asked about you at every cottage in He-Ping."

As the children told their sad story, the garden gate squeaked open. It was Baba.

"Now we're going to get whacked with the cane for sure," moaned Di-Di.

But as Baba drew nearer, they spied the glint of his gold tooth. His eyes were moist, but he was smiling! Even more surprising, he cradled a dove in his arms.

"Butterfly!" the children cried.

"She came home at dawn with a hurt wing. It'll mend," said Baba. He wiped his eyes. "Where were you? You nearly killed us with worry!"

"We're sorry, Baba," said Mei-Mei. "We went to Dog Willow to look for our doves."

"And I'm very sorry that I was too busy to see how much you loved them." Baba rubbed the tops of Mei-Mei's and Di-Di's heads. "You've taken care of them since they were babies, just as we've taken care of you."

As Baba, Mama, Mei-Mei, and Di-Di walked
back toward the house with Butterfly, Squeaky floated
down from the heavens in a burst of white and lit on
Di-Di's head.

"*Hen hao*—very good," Baba said. "You have all
come home."

And since that day, whenever the children

release their doves to the wind and sky, they still sing,

"*Fei, fei*—fly, fly, little birds, but always come home to us!"